My Best Friend
DUKE

Written and illustrated by:
Carrie Ludwick

authorHOUSE®

AuthorHouse™
1663 Liberty Drive
Bloomington, IN 47403
www.authorhouse.com
Phone: 1-800-839-8640

First published by AuthorHouse   02/20/2012

ISBN: 978-1-4685-5630-8 (sc)
ISBN: 978-1-4685-5631-5 (ebk)

Library of Congress Control Number: 2012903329

Printed in the United States of America

Any people depicted in stock imagery provided by Thinkstock are models, and such images are being used for illustrative purposes only.
Certain stock imagery © Thinkstock.

This book is printed on acid-free paper.

This is dedicated to Duke Oxford, Hunter's best and most trusted friend, forever.

In Memory of Hunter Johnson

February 4, 2000 - August 18, 2007

You and Me
Side by Side
Help each Other
When we cry

By Alexa Johnson

It was a great day to explore! The air was filled with the smells of cattails bursting open, leaves turning green, and geese flying home.

Duke knew the Universe Goose was watching out for them. Duke and his flock had been home for about a week. He was waiting for Hunter's flock to return.

Duke had known Hunter for years. They had met during gosling flight school.

Hunter was a giant Canada goose. His chest was white. His head was black with a white ribbon under his chin that wrapped up to his ears. His wings were waves of white, gray, and black. Hunter was larger than most Canada geese. His dad was a big goose too. Duke thought Hunter was a good-looking bird, but he wouldn't say that to anyone.

Duke was a snow goose. He looked just like his name sounded. He was all white, though for some reason, he had a metal band around one leg. He didn't remember how it got there. Hunter didn't have one.

Duke was up early that morning. At the cornfield, he heard from other geese that Hunter's flock should get in the next day. Oh, what a sight that would be, five hundred geese in a V formation. Geese stay in the V so they don't get lost. The geese behind the lead goose honk to the lead goose in support and encouragement. If the lead bird gets tired, then the next most experienced goose takes its place, and the flock gives him its honking support.

When male and female geese become mates, they stay together for life.

Duke flew straight home to tell his mother that Hunter's flock was due the next day. She had to plan a party. Duke wanted to serve pepperoni pizza, popcorn with M&M's, and grape punch. Oh, and donuts with sprinkles for dessert. Hunter's favorite. Mother made the list and gave Duke enough coin kernels to purchase the party supplies at the store.

Duke had learned so much from Hunter. Hunter knew everything. He knew how to set up the decoys so the city men hunted on the wrong lakes.

He could race a four-wheeler better than anyone else in town.

Hunter was the best video player ever. He knew how to play all the games. He could race around tracks faster than anyone, find targets quicker, and solve puzzles at the end of games.

He always won. Except when he played Duke, and then Duke won. Duke didn't understand why. He knew he wasn't as good as Hunter.

Duke did know that Hunter wasn't like the other fowl. He didn't go around squawking just for the sake of squawking. What he did was listen.

When he did speak, he told it like he saw it. Everyone knew how Hunter saw it. He was a real goose. He didn't blow smoke up any bird's feathers. He always told the truth. He told everyone how much he cared about them. Geese didn't tell one another how much they loved each other, but Duke loved Hunter like his own hatched brother.

Duke flew around the valley all night long. He went from the lake to the cornfield, from there to the four-wheeler track, and then back to the nest.

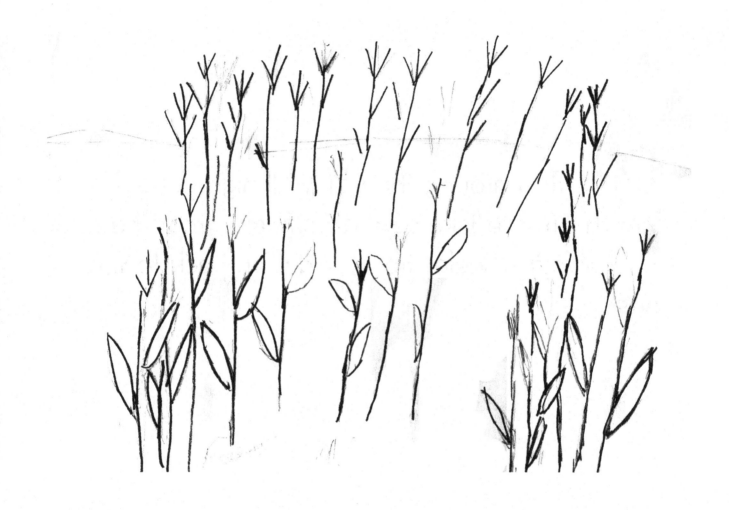

By the time the sun came up, he could barely move his wings. He wandered out onto the grassy field and fell asleep.

Duke felt something on his head. He shook his head, but whatever was on it, it did not move. He opened his eyes. A World Wind Hat stared back at him, and under the hat was Hunter. Duke jumped up, squawking and squawking.

"You're here, you're finally home! I've waited so long," he honked.

"Slow down," cried Hunter.

They talked and talked. Then out of nowhere Hunter said, "I need to get over to my nest."
"I'll come with you," said Duke.

"I'm sorry," Hunter said. "Can we do it tomorrow?"

"Yeah, sure. Okay, I'll see you then," answered Duke.

Hunter didn't even take off. He just walked away, one of his wings drooping. But he never said a thing.

As Hunter headed home, he flew over Duke's nest and he saw a sign that read Welcome Home.

Oh, no, he thought. He landed on the lake. Looking up into the heavens, he prayed: Dear Universe Goose, please help me. I need the strength to go back and be with Duke. I can't disappoint him. I love him. He will be so hurt. Please help me. Give me your love, support, and light. In your name I pray.

Hunter took off from the lake and landed at Duke's front door just as Duke arrived home.

"Hunter?" Duke honked. "I thought . . . ?"

"I couldn't let all of this go to waste now, could I, best friend?" Hunter said.

They played video games for hours, and of course Duke won.

The sun was coming up the next morning when Duke flew over to the cornfield. All the geese were making such noise.

"What's going on?" honked Duke.

Alexa, one of the geese in Hunter's flock, answered, "Hunter didn't lead formation yesterday."

"That's not true, he always leads!" Duke honked back, quite loudly.

"Well, he didn't!" she snapped.

Duke flew away. He had to find out about this. He spotted Hunter standing on the top of the lake ridge and flew down to him.

"Hey, bud, what's up?" he honked.

"Going down to take a swim," Hunter replied. "Need to wash off these dusty feathers."

"How was the lead home?" Duke asked as they flew down to the lake.

Hunter didn't turn to look at him. "Oh, I didn't lead. I gave Keygun a chance."

Duke didn't say anything else, but he knew something wasn't right.

After their swim, Hunter waddled up on the grass and started grooming his feathers. His feathers came out by the beak full.

"I sure am shedding this spring," he said.

Duke had never seen a Canada goose shed so much. There were feathers everywhere. "You sure are," he replied.

Both squatted down to rest.

When they woke up, Hunter said, "Let's go over to the track to ride the four-wheelers for the last time."

"What do you mean, the last time?" Duke honked in alarm.

"This week!" squawked Hunter.

They chased each other for hours. Hunter rode and rode. He didn't even take a break until the sun had long gone down.

He climbed off his four-wheeler and laughed. He squawked and squawked about how much fun he'd had. Then he asked Duke, "Hey, is there any of that pepperoni pizza left?"

As, they were flying to Duke's nest, Hunter said, "Duke, you know you're my best friend, don't you?"

"Sure I do," replied Duke.

"Good," honked Hunter. "I never want you to forget it!"

Hunter left after they ate. A few minutes later, Duke could swear he heard someone getting sick down the lane.

The next morning Duke slept in. When he got to the cornfield, he expected to see Hunter. Hunter wasn't there, and no one had seen him, even though it was already noon.

Hunter didn't come back till early evening.

"Hey, bud," honked Duke. "Where you been?"

"I had some things to do with my dad," Hunter said.

"You want to do something?" Duke asked.

"Nah, just swim awhile," chirped Hunter.

Chirped? thought Duke. What was this?

After about thirty minutes Hunter said, "Well, I'm a little tired. I'm going up to the nest. See you tomorrow."

Duke watched him fly away in disbelief. Something was wrong with Hunter. He had to get to the bottom of this. He went looking for his dad.

He knew the older geese would be up at the cattails at this time of day. Hunter's dad would be there, too, so he could shoot two tails with one shot. He flew toward the lake and spotted his dad with Hunter's dad, Mr. R. J. Goose. He hovered over the lake. The two older geese were in a deep conversation.

Duke landed and squawked at his dad. His dad came toward him, as did R.J. Goose.

"What's wrong with Hunter?" Duke honked. "He's not himself. He's doing weird stuff. His feathers are falling out." Duke was shaking all over, right down to his webbed feet.

"I know, Duke," R.J. honked as he turned away. Duke's dad put his wing around him.

"Son," Duke's dad said, "Hunter's gone."

"No, I have to find him," Duke squawked, louder than before.

Flying as fast as he could, he looked for Hunter at the cornfield, and then at the four-wheeler track, and finally back at the lake.

He didn't find Hunter, but he could not fly anymore. He landed on the lake and swam back into the tall weeds. He didn't want anyone to see him. He tucked his head beneath his wing. He cried so hard, he could barely stay afloat. He knew Hunter was gone forever.

As he floated there, a strange sensation came over him. It was warmer than the sun, fresh, cleansing, and uplifting. He pulled his head from beneath his wing.

Surrounding him was a great light. It made his feathers shimmer, like they were covered in silver glitter. He heard a voice like none he'd ever heard before.

"I shall bring you peace, love, and trust in me. You shall be together again." The light drifted up into the heavens.

Duke felt peace. He did love. And he and Hunter were together again.